G.I. JOE AT D-DAY

LOOK FOR THESE OTHER G.I. JOE BOOKS:

G.I. JOE

G.I. JOE
AT
D-DAY

James Kelley

SCHOLASTIC INC.
New York Toronto London Auckland Sydney

ISBN 0-590-14976-8

12 11 10 9 8 7 6 5   3/0

Printed in the U.S.A.

First Scholastic printing, March 1998

This book is dedicated to every G.I. Joe who didn't come home from D-Day.

Contents

G.I. JOE

AT

D-DAY

CROSS SECTION
OF OMAHA BEACH

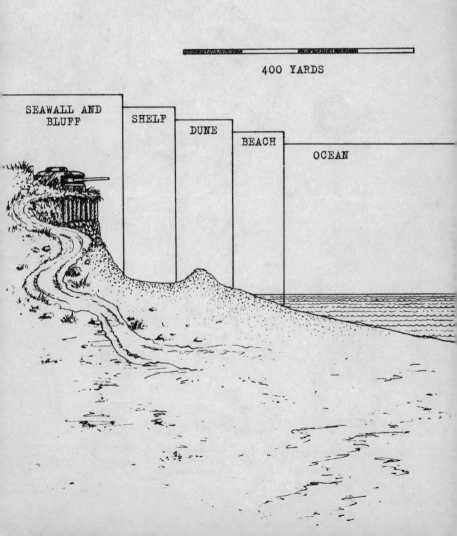

400 YARDS

SEAWALL AND BLUFF

SHELF

DUNE

BEACH

OCEAN

DOG TAGS

FIRED
CARTRIDGES

HAND TORCH TL122-C

8 ROUND CLIP OF
.30 CALIBER M1
RIFLE AMMUNITION

G.I.JOE®

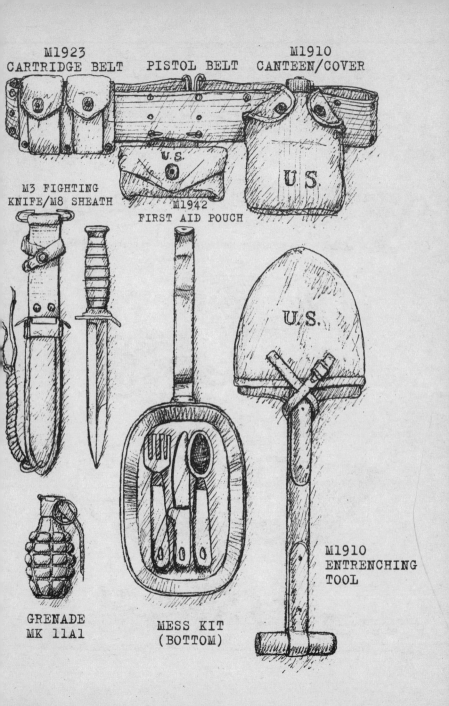

M1923
CARTRIDGE BELT   PISTOL BELT

M1910
CANTEEN/COVER

U.S.

U.S.

M3 FIGHTING
KNIFE/M8 SHEATH

M1942
FIRST AID POUCH

U.S.

GRENADE
MK 11A1

MESS KIT
(BOTTOM)

M1910
ENTRENCHING
TOOL

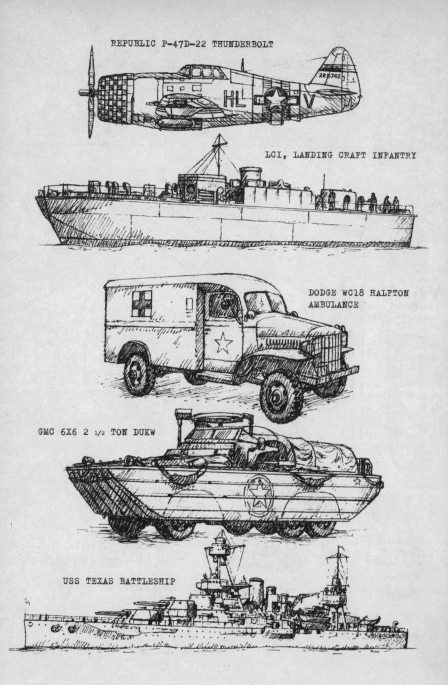

REPUBLIC P-47D-22 THUNDERBOLT

LCI, LANDING CRAFT INFANTRY

DODGE WC18 HALFTON
AMBULANCE

GMC 6X6 2 1/2 TON DUKW

USS TEXAS BATTLESHIP

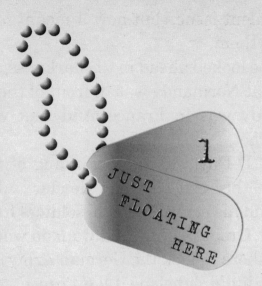

JUST
FLOATING
HERE

1

Midnight, June 6, 1944. In a few hours, G.I. Joe and his squad were about to begin the biggest and most important battle of World War II.

G.I. Joe sat on a ship floating in the English Channel. He looked out into the inky midnight darkness. And he couldn't see a thing.

It is really dark out here, he thought.

G.I. Joe and his buddies were on a big ship filled with thousands of other soldiers. They were all G.I.s. G.I. used to mean "government issue," but now it meant men just like them.

G.I. Joe looked ahead in the darkness. He knew that Normandy was in front of them. Normandy was in France. And that was their target.

Today, D-Day, was the beginning of the end for the evil German leader Adolf Hitler and his army. At dawn, soldiers from America, Great Britain, and Canada would storm ashore to kick the German Army out of places it didn't belong. Like France.

G.I. Joe heard a voice. It came from one of the other soldiers squeezed onto the deck of the ship.

"I feel like a sardine," "Sleepy" Steve Nelson said, shifting his shoulders to get more space. Steve had earned his nickname during training when he dozed off during a first-aid lesson given by the most boring teacher in the Army.

"A sardine in a tin can has more room," Marco Martino answered.

"And smells better," Arnold "Wheeze" Russell added. He was right. A ship full of sweaty men and a smoky engine didn't smell like roses.

The weather had calmed down a bit by midnight. *Thank goodness,* thought G.I. Joe.

All the way across the English Channel, which was between England and France, the ship had been bounced up and down through the rough water. The ride had made all the men seasick!

Among those men were G.I. Joe and his buddies — Marco, Sleepy Steve, Wheeze, and the others. They had become like brothers since their squad of a dozen men was formed.

The squad was part of a larger Army unit called the 1st Infantry Division. The division of 14,000 men was also called the Big Red One, after the patch they wore on their shirts.

Lt. Tim Seeberg was in command of several squads. G.I. Joe's squad itself was led by Sgt. Morty Davidson. He was so big and powerful, he looked like a refrigerator wearing a helmet.

"I hate the name Morty," the sergeant said when they met him. "Just call me Big D."

"He's not just Big D," Marco had joked after the sergeant was out of hearing. "He's Big A, B, C, *and* D."

G.I. Joe himself was a private, the lowest rank in the Army, but he was part of a great team. Joe knew the squad would back him up in battle. And he would try to back them up. Teamwork was the key to being a good soldier.

"You worried?" Sleepy Steve asked his buddy from the darkness.

"A little bit, Sleepy," G.I. Joe said. "But we've got the best equipment, and we're well trained. I think we'll be all right."

"I don't know. This attack sounds dangerous."

"Hey, we signed up for dangerous work. And we've got a job to do," G.I. Joe said.

"Hey, blabbermouths," Big D hissed. "You want the Germans to hear you? Keep your lips zipped!"

G.I. Joe patted the pockets of his dark green shirt, looking for a candy bar. His hands touched some paper in his top pocket.

Darn it, he thought. *That's my letter home. I should have mailed that before we left England.*

G.I. Joe and the other soldiers hadn't been able to send any mail for several weeks, because D-Day was such a secret. But just before they got on the ships to France, the soldiers were allowed to write one letter.

G.I. Joe wrote to his mom and told her about their training in England, and about the guys in his squad. He told her not to worry, even though he knew she would.

It was an important letter.

Except he forgot to mail it.

5

I hope Mom doesn't get too worried, he thought. He put the letter into a plastic bag.

Don't want this to get wet. Maybe I can mail it when I get to France. I'll get some French stamps. Mom will like that.

As G.I. Joe sat in the darkness, munching on a candy bar, he thought back to the road he had traveled to get here.

2
HOW WE GOT HERE

G.I. Joe had been in England for the three months before D-Day. He had learned a lot of things. But what he would remember most was mystery meat and marmalade.

During their training for the battle, Joe and his buddies had the same lunch almost every day: a slice of mystery meat and a blob of fruity marmalade on thick slices of bread.

"If I never see another piece of whatever the heck this is my whole life, I'll be a happy man," Wheeze moaned one day.

"I'm going to become a vegetarian when this is over," said Marco.

"What is this stuff, anyway?" asked Johnny Parker, a soldier from Brooklyn known to everyone as J.P.

"Trust me," said Carl "Corny" Cornwall, a squad member from Nebraska. "You don't want to know."

G.I. Joe's squad trained hard in England. There was a lot to learn before they could go to France. They practiced beach landings, and they climbed rope ladders over and over. They learned about German defenses and took target practice with their rifles.

One of the things the men practiced was carrying each other piggy-back. G.I. Joe didn't know it then, but that training would come in handy on June 6.

Day after day, the soldiers practiced until they could make all the right moves in their sleep.

The men in G.I. Joe's squad weren't alone. More than one million soldiers from

England, America, and Canada were crowded into England, getting ready for D-Day. The soldiers filled every inn, every hotel, and every empty bed all over England.

And they ate a lot of mystery meat and marmalade.

One evening in early June, the men left the cook tent together after dinner. Marco and Wheeze found some baseball gloves and a ball and played catch in front of the tents where the men slept.

G.I. Joe, J.P., Corny, and Big D sat in front of the tents, enjoying a quiet evening after a hard day's work.

"Man, my legs are so sore, I don't think I can reach to untie my combat boots," Corny moaned.

"You're lucky you have boots," Big D said, munching on an apple. "There are people all over Europe without boots or shoes or anything. And all thanks to that rotten Hitler and the German Army."

"Do you think we can beat them, Sarge?" J.P. asked.

"No doubt about it," Big D snorted. "We're the best. We're right and he's wrong. That's all there is to it."

"That won't make it any easier," G.I. Joe said, frowning. *I just hope I have the strength I'll need when the time comes,* Joe thought.

The next day, Sgt. Davidson made all the guys in the squad check the equipment they would carry to France.

Each soldier carried an M-1 rifle. It was made of wood, with a metal barrel and trigger.

In their backpacks, the soldiers put tin cans of food called K rations, a compass, a first-aid kit, and spare socks and underwear. They strapped a short shovel to the back of the pack, and tied a sleeping bag on top.

Over a green Army shirt, each man wore

a canvas vest. It had pockets that the soldiers filled with all sorts of things.

"Look what some guy gave me," Marco said, pulling a piece of white cloth from one pocket. "It's a map of Normandy printed on silk. That way if it gets wet, it won't get ruined."

"I got a book of French words," Corny said. "That way I can talk to the farmers over there in Normandy."

They filled their canteens with water, and they found room for candy bars in their pockets. Sleepy Steve put a baseball in the bottom of his pack, just in case they got a chance to play.

No one carried a wallet, but each soldier put some special Army money and some French francs into one of his pockets.

The men were quiet as they checked their dog tags, the metal discs that hung on chains around their neck. In case they were injured, the tags told doctors who the soldiers were. The G.I.s all hoped they wouldn't need their dog tags.

Back on the boat on June 6, G.I. Joe fingered his dog tags as he remembered his time in England. Suddenly, Lt. Seeberg started yelling.

"On your feet! Let's go!"

This is it! G.I. Joe thought, scrambling to his feet. He heard the other soldiers getting up, too, their equipment rattling.

Lt. Seeberg and Sgt. Davidson ordered the squad to move to the edge of the ship. They got in line with hundreds of other soldiers, all dressed in green with their helmets strapped under their chins.

G.I. Joe felt like he was lining up to go into a football game. But this was no game. This was real.

The squad reached the front of the line.

"Okay, you lazy bums, nap time's over," Big D yelled as he climbed over the side of the ship. "Follow me!"

Joe and the others stepped over the side of the big ship and grabbed hold of the rope ladders that led down to the ocean.

It must be forty feet down to the water, G.I. Joe thought.

"Just hold tight," Sgt. Davidson said from below. "This is just like we practiced, remember?"

G.I. Joe nodded and climbed over the side. The sergeant was right; G.I. Joe *knew* he could do this!

Sgt. Davidson and the others looked like spiders climbing backward down the big web of rope on the side of the ship.

As each man reached the bottom, he dropped onto the deck of a smaller boat that would take them to the beach. This small boat was an LCI — Landing Craft, Infantry.

When everyone was aboard, Lt. Seeberg turned to the LCI pilot.

"All right," he shouted, "Let's get going."

In the LCI, which looked like a giant

metal shoebox with no lid, the men huddled together for warmth in the chilly night air.

It was just after 4 A.M.

D-Day was about to start.

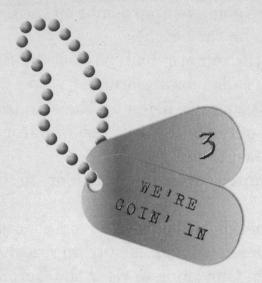

3

WE'RE
GOIN' IN

As the LCI started moving slowly toward the beach, the men heard a loud buzzing sound overhead that got louder and louder.

They looked up, but they couldn't see through the heavy fog.

"What the heck is all that noise?" Corny yelled, his fingers in his ears.

"That's the sweetest sound I've heard all day," Sgt. Davidson yelled. "Those are our planes, heading for France."

He was right. Thousands of airplanes were headed for the coastline of Normandy.

They were going to drop bombs on the German forts on the beaches.

After the planes had passed by, Sgt. Davidson called for attention.

"Okay, you guys, listen up," he said from the front of the boat. "Let's review our mission one last time."

He pointed over his shoulder to the beach.

"The beach we're landing on is code-named Omaha. There is only one road off the beach. Our job is to clear the German Army off that road. Our part of the beach is code-named Dog Green. You can't see it now, but that road is there, believe me."

The sergeant paused, scratching his chin.

"Guys, I won't kid you," he continued. "This ain't gonna be easy. Those Germans don't want to give up this nice beach to a bunch of Americans. But that's what we're here to do and that's what we're *gonna* do!"

The men all shouted in agreement. "We're with you, Sarge!"

"Now, let's make sure to work together, keep our heads down, and do the things we've trained to do," Sgt. Davidson said.

He looked at his watch. "Okay, guys, we've got about an hour or so before anything happens. Try to find a comfortable spot and get some rest. You won't see your sleeping bag until midnight . . . and that's a long time from now."

G.I. Joe and the squad tried to sit down in the LCI, but it was pretty crowded. Besides, everyone was too excited and nervous to sleep.

G.I. Joe went over the mission in his head one last time.

When the front door of this LCI opens, we run as fast as we can for the beach. Then we head for the seawall at the back of the beach. Sounds easy, huh? It probably won't be.

"What's it like? Battle, I mean?" Wheeze asked, interrupting G.I. Joe's thoughts. G.I. Joe had been in some small battles before, but nothing as huge as D-Day.

"It's loud, for one thing," G.I. Joe said. "And it happens fast. You just have to remember all the training we did and let your instincts take over."

The men were quiet for a while. They checked their equipment and listened to more planes fly overhead.

They bobbed in the floating shoe box for about an hour, growing more nervous. They slowly moved closer to the beach.

Curiously, the German Army didn't shoot at them.

"Maybe they've all gone back to Germany," Marco said.

"Don't count on it," Lt. Seeberg said. "They're just waiting until we're closer."

Slowly, the sun came up. In the early morning light, the soldiers could see the wide, white beach with broad dunes. At the back of the beach was a wood and stone seawall in front of a small hill.

G.I. Joe pointed to a spot amid the dunes. "Is that Dog Green, Sarge?" he asked.

"Good eye," the sergeant said. "Yep, that's Dog Green. And that's the road we have to open."

The men could see a narrow road leading off the beach. It looked peaceful enough, lined with waving sea grass. They saw a church steeple farther inland. There were even a few houses.

Just then, the sound of a thousand thunders pounded into their ears. BOOM! BOOM! BOOM! over and over and over. The men covered their ears and ducked their heads.

"Now it's the Navy's turn!" Wheeze shouted over the noise. "They're sending more bombs at the Germans."

"I hope those guys on the beach get the message," Corny said.

"If they don't, I got another message for them here," Marco said, patting his rifle.

The booming continued. Then the LCI began to pick up speed. The beach got closer and closer.

"This is it!" G.I. Joe shouted.

The LCI went faster and faster! The booming got louder and louder!

Then, suddenly, the LCI slammed to a halt in the sand just offshore.

Sgt. Davidson, G.I. Joe, Marco, J.P., Wheeze, Sleepy Steve, Corny, and the others gathered at the front of the boat. Lt. Seeberg was right behind them with another squad.

The giant door at the front of the LCI splashed into the water! Shouting and yelling, the men started out toward the beach, their guns held high.

D-Day had begun.

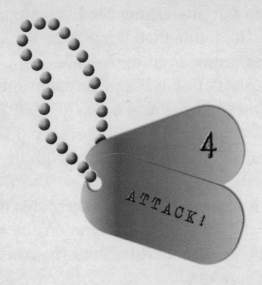

4

ATTACK!

Sgt. Davidson led the squad into the water.

"Let's go! Hit the beach!"

And at that moment, the German guns started blasting away at them!

Bullets zinged off the metal sides of the LCI. Giant towers of water burst into the air as bombs landed. The air was filled with smoke and noise. Bright orange flashes lit up the small hills at the back of the beach.

G.I. Joe felt something hit his arm, as if someone had punched him. But he kept going and jumped out of the LCI.

Suddenly G.I. Joe found himself underwater. The Channel was much deeper than they had thought! Loaded down by all his equipment, he struggled to swim in his bulky boots.

After a few sputtering dog paddles, G.I. Joe and the others could stand on the bottom. They held their rifles over their heads to keep them dry.

The noise got louder and louder. Bombs were crashing all around them. They heard the *chat-chat-chatter* of machine guns.

The seawall seemed very far away. G.I. Joe knew they had to reach it to do their job.

But they would have to get there one step at a time.

"Don't stop, no matter what!" G.I. Joe yelled as he waded forward.

Sgt. Davidson pointed with his rifle toward a big dune in the beach in front of them. It looked like a good place to stop and get organized.

"Let's try to go there first!" the Sarge yelled.

As G.I. Joe turned to wave his buddies on after the sergeant, he saw Corny stop moving. Corny got a strange look on his face. Then the young farm boy disappeared under the water.

Corny wouldn't be going back to Nebraska.

G.I. Joe grimaced, but he kept going toward the beach.

Ahead of him, he saw giant steel beams sticking out of the sand, forming giant Xs. The beams had been put there to stop boats and tanks from rolling ashore. With the tide low, they also were good to hide behind.

But not good enough. G.I. Joe got to the first set of the beams and saw Sleepy Steve and Marco crouched there.

"You can't stay here all day," G.I. Joe shouted over the roar of the bombs.

Marco looked up as the water from a wave splashed his legs. His eyes were wide with fear.

"I can't go on!" he yelled. "I can't move! I'm scared!"

"I know — we all are!" G.I. Joe shouted, and pushed the two men forward, up the beach. "But if you stay here, you'll be underwater soon. Head for dry ground!"

A huge blast knocked G.I. Joe off his feet. But he didn't stay down. He climbed to his feet, strapped his helmet back on, and kept going.

Big D was yelling at other men in the water to move onto the beach. They sloshed and splashed and tripped in the wet sand, but they kept moving.

G.I. Joe saw Lt. Seeberg run up the beach to help one of his other squads. Then he disappeared amid the smoke.

G.I. Joe looked up and down the beach. Thousands more soldiers just like him were streaming ashore from other LCIs. The thousands of men looked like a wide green wave heading toward the German Army. Joe hoped the wave would wash the German Army away forever.

He kept running up the beach, heading for the large dune so they could regroup. The noise was incredible. G.I. Joe couldn't believe how hard this was!

So many guns were firing at the Americans that the hills behind the beach looked like a wall of flame. G.I. Joe looked ahead and saw three soldiers lying still on the sand. G.I. Joe looked away.

Just a few more yards, he thought, *just a few more feet.* His big boots churned in the sand.

He dove through the air into the sand. He rolled toward the bottom of the big dune. With his back to the dune, he was hidden and safe — for now — from the German guns. The rest of the squad saw G.I. Joe and kept charging up the beach to join him.

Big D fell into the sand next to G.I. Joe, breathing hard.

"C'mon, you guys," he yelled, waving the men on. "Up here!"

They saw Marco and Sleepy Steve racing toward them. The two soldiers dove into the sand and crawled the last few yards.

"Thanks, pal," Marco said. "I'd still be down there if you hadn't come by."

"Just helpin' out," G.I. Joe said. "We gotta stick together, remember?"

A few more guys from the squad crowded behind the dune. The dune was the only cover until the seawall, fifty yards farther inland.

"Where's J.P.?" Marco asked.

They looked around in the crowd of men, but didn't see their buddy from Brooklyn.

"There he is," Big D said. He pointed out toward the steel tank traps, sticking up like broken toys from the sand.

J.P. lay near the bottom of one of them. His helmet was off, and he wasn't moving.

Wheeze put his face in his hands.

G.I. Joe touched the letter home that was still in his pocket.

The squad talked about what to do next.

"We can't stay here all day," Sgt. Davidson said.

"We need to get moving," Marco agreed. "The seawall isn't much farther. Once we reach that, we can try to capture the road."

"I think we can make it," G.I. Joe said.

Joe looked around at the men huddled against the dune. They were soaking wet, covered with sand, and scared. The noise from the German guns went on and on. And they had already lost two of their buddies.

No one wanted to leave the safety of the dune. But deep down inside, G.I. Joe and the others knew they had to keep going. They couldn't come all this way and just stop.

"Guys, I'm proud of you for coming this far," Sgt. Davidson said in a loud voice. "But we haven't gone far enough. This day's just starting."

"But what about Corny and J.P.!" Wheeze shouted angrily, tears forming in his eyes.

"Hey!" G.I. Joe said sharply. "Enough of that! They were the best, but they wouldn't want you to give up. There are millions of people counting on us. And we're not going to save anyone sitting on this beach."

Sgt. Davidson looked at G.I. Joe proudly.

"He's right, guys," Sgt. Davidson said, standing up slowly.

Big D smiled, and his teeth were bright white on his dark-bearded, sand-covered, sweaty face.

"Let's go!" With that yell, he charged over the top of the dune, blasting away with his rifle.

G.I. Joe looked at his sergeant running up the beach. He knew he had to follow. G.I. Joe told his tired legs to move, even though they wanted to rest.

G.I. Joe repeated the Sarge's yell as loudly as he could.

"C'mon! Let's go!"

The other men joined in and charged forward. Toward the German Army.

Their time-out was over.

The battle was on.

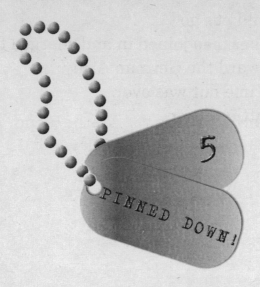

5

PINNED DOWN!

The squad poured over the edge of the dune together. Big D was in the lead, shouting and firing his gun as he ran. Marco, Wheeze, and Sleepy Steve were behind him. They churned through the soft sand toward the high seawall at the back of Omaha Beach.

G.I. Joe ran with them. He tripped and fell once, falling behind the others.

Bursts of sand kicked up all around him, as German guns fired all around. Bombs landed nearby, throwing stinging sand at him. G.I. Joe tried to wipe his face as he ran. But one eye filled with sand.

He looked ahead fuzzily as he ran. He could hardly see through the sand and smoke. Had the sergeant fallen, too?

The others ran on ahead, toward the safety of the seawall. But G.I. Joe saw Big D struggling to get up. Now the sand in G.I. Joe's eyes was getting scratchier. He couldn't see his boots as he kept running.

Wham!

G.I. Joe tripped over something and fell face-first into the sand.

Blindly, he felt around for his rifle, but he grabbed a boot instead.

"Who's there?" he shouted over the roar of the cannons.

"It's me," Big D yelled, "I'm hit. You go on."

"No way, Sarge, I'm not leaving you here. C'mon, on your feet."

"I can't. My leg is hurt, can't you see that?"

31

The sergeant looked up at G.I. Joe, whose face was covered in wet sand.

"Actually, Sarge, I can't see a thing."

"Well, just turn around and get going, darn it!" Sarge yelled. "I'm just going to slow you down. Start running until you hit the wall."

"No can do, Sarge," G.I. Joe said. "Tell you what. I'll be your legs and you be my eyes. Just like we practiced in England."

Joe couldn't leave the sergeant behind, even though he wanted to be safe.

Joe lifted his sergeant onto his powerful back.

"Okay, Sarge," G.I. Joe said. "Which way do we go?"

"Take two steps to your right, then go as fast as you can," Big D shouted over the sound of the guns. "And hurry! These German bullets are getting close."

G.I. Joe started running. The piggy-backing pair bounced and staggered across the sand.

"To the left!" Sarge shouted when they neared a big bomb crater.

"To the right!" he yelled when they got near a giant log.

"Take a big jump forward," he told G.I. Joe when they got near a dip in the sand.

Finally, the two-man team reached the rest of the squad at the seawall. G.I. Joe lowered the sergeant gently to the beach. They put their backs to the wall and stopped to catch their breath.

Joe got out his canteen and finally washed the sand out of his eyes.

"That's better," he said. "Now I can see."

But what he saw didn't make him happy. On Omaha Beach, he saw burning tanks, crashed LCIs, and wounded men. More boats were jammed up, heading to shore.

Big D turned on the radio that he carried. The men listened to reports from other D-Day landing sites. The armies of three countries had landed together and were beginning to take back Europe.

Canadian and British voices reported from beaches code-named Gold, Juno, and Sword. An American voice spoke from Utah Beach. They all were headed inland, while the men on Omaha were stuck here in the sand.

"Sounds like we got the toughest job of all," Sleepy Steve said. "Just our luck Omaha would be a hard nut to crack."

"That's why they sent us, Steve," G.I. Joe said. After carrying the sergeant, he felt stronger and braver. He felt as if he could take on anything and anyone.

Lt. Seeberg still hadn't joined them. So Sgt. Davidson spoke into the radio microphone. "Davidson to Omaha HQ, come in."

The radio crackled back at him. "Go ahead, Davidson, what is your situation?"

"At the seawall, preparing to attack Dog Green. Over."

"You must take Dog Green soon," the voice on the radio said. "We need to get our men off the beach as soon as possible."

"Got it," Sgt. Davidson replied. "We're on our way. Over and out." He slipped the radio back into his pack. Big D couldn't wait for orders from Lt. Seeberg. They were on their own.

"Marco! Hey, Marco," the sergeant yelled. "Take two guys with you and scout up the road a bit. Let us know what's up there."

"Gotcha, Sarge," Marco said. They edged around the wall, and began to walk slowly up the road. In a moment, they had disappeared from view.

As the squad waited for the others, they heard a high whistling sound overhead. Then there were dozens of loud BOOMS!

"It's the *Frankford*!" shouted Wheeze. The soldiers looked out to sea. They could see bursts of yellow and orange coming from the big U.S. Navy destroyer *Frankford*. The ship was firing at the German guns.

G.I. Joe could hear cheers up and down the beach. It was good to have more teammates in the fight.

But the fight wasn't over ... not even close.

Suddenly, they heard the deadly chatter of a German machine gun! It was coming from the road where Marco had gone!

A few nervous seconds passed until Marco stumbled around the corner from the road. He was holding his shoulder and limping. He fell with a cry of pain into the sand.

G.I. Joe and Wheeze leaped to their feet and hauled Marco to the safety of the seawall.

"Marco!" Wheeze yelled into Marco's ear. "Marco! Can you hear me?"

"Of course I can hear ya, ya bonehead, I'm lyin' right here." But the men weren't fooled by Marco's joking. He was bleeding from two bullet wounds. A medic came over and began to patch him up.

"Sarge, I got bad news," Marco said as the medic worked on him. "There's a German machine gun at the top of the road. We're not going anywhere!"

He pointed to the rest of the U.S. Army running up Omaha Beach toward the road. "And neither are they.

"We're pinned down!"

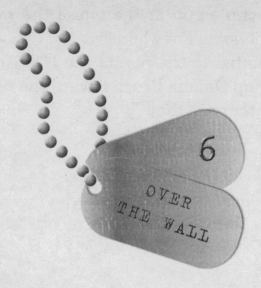

6

OVER THE WALL

While bombs from the *Frankford* whistled overhead, the other troops advanced up the beach. Soon they would be stuck at Dog Green, with no place to go. They'd be sitting ducks.

The men of G.I. Joe's squad knew they would have to charge up that road in a minute. They had to knock out the machine gun to make the road safe. It would be very dangerous. They had studied the German defenses and knew that the machine guns were usually in strong, concrete buildings that the Germans had built.

Then G.I. Joe had an idea.

"Sarge," he said. "There's no way we can take that machine gun head on. But maybe there's another way. If you can get me to the top of this hill, maybe I can sneak around behind the gun and take it out."

Big D looked at the man who had just carried him across the battlefield. He was proud of G.I. Joe. Being in this battle had made him stronger. But not taller. The wall rose up about twenty feet over their heads to the top of the hill. And they didn't have a ladder.

Then Big D snapped his fingers. "I've got an idea, too."

While G.I. Joe strapped on his helmet, the sergeant got the other men together.

"That's right, Wheeze," the sergeant said. "Sleepy Steve goes up on your shoulders. Put your back up against the wall."

Steve climbed onto Wheeze's shoulders. Both men's backs were to the wall.

"Okay, kid, up you go," Big D said. "I'll give you three minutes from when you get to the top."

"Got it, Sarge," G.I. Joe said.

Marco's eyes got wide as he realized what G.I. Joe was going to do.

"Hey, wait a minute, buddy," he said, lying in the sand. "You can't go up there alone."

"I won't be alone, Marco," G.I. Joe said. "I need you guys to distract that machine gun."

"But . . ." Marco started to argue.

"It's okay, Marco," G.I. Joe said. "Trust me."

And with that, G.I. Joe climbed up the human ladder formed by Wheeze and Sleepy Steve.

Joe reached the top of the wall that held up the hill. He saw nothing but tall green grass atop the hill. It was nice and flat. *Perfect,* he thought. *No German guards.*

From below, Sgt. Davidson watched G.I. Joe pull himself over the top of the seawall and disappear. Then Sgt. Davidson checked his watch. He started the three-minute countdown.

"Okay, you guys," he yelled. "When I say GO! aim your rifles up the road and give that machine gun everything you've got!"

"But Sarge," Wheeze complained. "That thing's solid concrete! It's like throwing spitwads at a brick wall."

"I know that, but I want them looking down the road, not at our teammate up there."

Atop the hill, G.I. Joe lay flat on his stomach. Covered by the grass, he was invisible to the Germans. He began to crawl slowly toward them.

He reached a scrawny tree. He peeked around to see how much farther he had to go. As he did, he also checked his watch.

Two minutes to go.

He began to crawl again. He was trying

to reach the back door of the concrete building that housed the machine gun.

He could hear shooting from the beach as German guns all over Omaha aimed at the rest of the Big Red One coming ashore. There was no place for those troops to go. That machine gun was like the cork in a bottle. If it didn't come out, the troops would be stuck on the beach! He had to get that road open!

Slithering through the tall grass, G.I. Joe moved slowly toward the German gunners. He was getting so close, he could hear them talking.

One minute to go.

Suddenly, through a break in the grass, G.I. Joe saw what he was looking for. The German soldiers had to get in the building somehow, and there was the wooden door! The wall all around was concrete. He couldn't get through that. But a wooden door, well, that was nothing for a G.I. And there were no guards!

Thirty seconds.

I hope this works, G.I. Joe thought. *A lot of guys are depending on us to get this road open.*

He slid a few feet closer. He could see the doorknob. They're expecting trouble from the front, not from this side. He checked his watch.

Ten seconds.

Sgt. Davidson was watching the second hand on his watch.

Five seconds. Four! Three! Two! One!

"GO! GO! GO!" he shouted.

The men aimed up the road, and blasted away at the concrete building.

From their mini-fort, the Germans shot back down the road. Inside, the noise was incredible. They couldn't hear a thing.

That was what G.I. Joe was counting on.

As soon as he heard his buddies start shooting, he jumped up and ran to the wooden door.

Raising up one big boot, he kicked the door in!

BLAM! The door flew off its hinges, wood splintering everywhere.

G.I. Joe burst into the room, yelling at the top of his lungs!

"Put 'em up!" he shouted, pointing his rifle. "That's it!"

The Germans had no time to react. They dropped their weapons and put up their hands. G.I. Joe took away their guns and helmets. He pointed to the door.

"Let's go," he said. "Your war is over."

He led the German prisoners out of the concrete fort. As he came around the front, the rest of the squad was charging up the road, cheering!

"We did it!" Marco yelled. "We did it!"

"The road is open!" Sleepy Steve shouted.

Behind the men of G.I. Joe's squad, thousands of other U.S. soldiers began to race up Dog Green. The parade of men, tanks, trucks, and jeeps would go on for days.

D-Day was a success!

7

THE END OF THE DAY

Several hours later, G.I. Joe's squad sat by the side of the Dog Green road, eating their rations and watching the Army pass by. Once the squad — led by G.I. Joe's bravery — had cleared away the machine gun, the other Germans in the area headed inland.

The squad was happy. They knew that without their hard work, the parade of soldiers they were watching never would have happened.

The memory of their friends J.P. and Corny was with them. And Marco and Sgt. Davidson would soon be headed back to England to get better. They would miss those guys, too.

"Man, you're a hero!" Wheeze said to G.I. Joe between bites. "I still can't believe what you did. You took on that machine gun single-handed!"

G.I. Joe sat down on a rock and pushed his helmet back.

"Thanks, Wheeze," he said. "But you know I couldn't have done it without you guys. Together, we made a big change in the battle."

"Can we change our clothes, too?" Sleepy Steve joked. "I've got enough sand in my pockets to start my own beach."

It was good to be able to laugh, even at dumb jokes.

And it was good to hear more reports from other beaches.

D-Day had become one of history's greatest examples of teamwork. Three countries worked together. Thousands of people in England had cared for the soldiers during training. In America, millions of people in factories had made the gear, vehicles, and food that the soldiers needed.

It was a team effort. Now, all over Europe, the people who had been conquered by the German Army had new hope.

World War II wouldn't end for another year. But the beginning of the end was D-Day. And D-Day was a success because of brave men like G.I. Joe and his buddies.

An ambulance pulled up beside the squad. Big D called to them from inside.

"Hey, you guys," he said. "You think you can take back France without me?"

The squad would soon march inland with the rest of the Big Red One. They had to push the German Army all the way back to Germany.

Now, the men crowded around the ambulance to shake hands with Sgt. Davidson and Marco.

"We'll sure try, Sarge," G.I. Joe said. "Without you, we wouldn't have made it this far. You just go back and get better."

"Listen, Joe, I talked to Lt. Seeberg," Big D said, reaching into his pocket. "These are for you."

The men all cheered as Sgt. Davidson handed Joe a green and yellow patch with three stripes. G.I. Joe was now a sergeant.

"You're in charge until I get back, Sarge," Big D said. "Keep up the good work."

"Thanks," G.I. Joe said proudly. "I'll do my best."

The men waved to Big D and Marco as they drove off.

"Hey, you guys are the best," Marco called out. "If you're ever in San Francisco, stop by my parents' restaurant. No mystery meat, I promise!"

The men watched as the ambulance pulled away.

Then G.I. Joe remembered something and ran down the hill to catch the ambulance.

"Hey, Sarge," he said, pulling open the ambulance door and reaching into his pocket. "Can you do me a favor?"

"After what you did for me on that beach, I'd do anything for you. Just name it."

"Can you mail this letter for me? It's for my mom, and I forgot to mail it before I left."

Sgt. Davidson took the letter, still wrapped in plastic. He buttoned it into his shirt pocket.

"There aren't enough German soldiers in the world to stop me from mailing this letter."

The two friends shook hands. Then the ambulance moved off.

Sergeant G.I. Joe picked up his rifle and put on his helmet and backpack. And he began to walk up the road.

D-Day was ending, but there was still a war to win.